This book belongs to

KAY CHORAO

Rhymes Round

the World

Dutton Children's Books

For Katie, Jameson, Malcolm, and Sadie,
whose roots stretch round the world

DUTTON CHILDREN'S BOOKS
A division of Penguin Young Readers Group

Published by the Penguin Group
Penguin Group (USA) Inc., 375 Hudson Street, New York, New York 10014, U.S.A.
Penguin Group (Canada), 90 Eglinton Avenue East, Suite 700, Toronto, Ontario, Canada M4P 2Y3 (a division of Pearson Penguin Canada Inc.)
Penguin Books Ltd, 80 Strand, London WC2R 0RL, England
Penguin Ireland, 25 St Stephen's Green, Dublin 2, Ireland (a division of Penguin Books Ltd)
Penguin Group (Australia), 250 Camberwell Road, Camberwell, Victoria 3124, Australia (a division of Pearson Australia Group Pty Ltd)
Penguin Books India Pvt Ltd, 11 Community Centre, Panchsheel Park, New Delhi - 110 017, India
Penguin Group (NZ), 67 Apollo Drive, Rosedale, North Shore 0632, New Zealand (a division of Pearson New Zealand Ltd)
Penguin Books (South Africa) (Pty) Ltd, 24 Sturdee Avenue, Rosebank, Johannesburg 2196, South Africa
Penguin Books Ltd, Registered Offices: 80 Strand, London WC2R 0RL, England

Every attempt has been made to trace the ownership of all copyrighted material and to secure the necessary permissions
to reprint these selections. In the event of any question arising as to the use of any material, the editor and the publisher,
while expressing regret for any inadvertent error, will be happy to make the necessary correction in future printings.
The publisher gratefully acknowledges the right to reprint:

"Little Pine" from MAPLES IN THE MIST: Children's Poems from the Tang Dynasty, adapted by Minfong Ho,
published by Lothrop, Lee & Shepard. Copyright 1996 by Minfong Ho. Reprinted by permission of McIntosh & Otis, Inc.

"Tickle Tickle" from the collection IN DADDY'S ARMS I AM TALL: AFRICAN AMERICANS CELEBRATING FATHERS,
text copyright © 1997 by Dakari Hru. Permission arranged with Lee & Low Books, New York, NY 10016.

"Wind Last Night" from SUNSET IN A SPIDER WEB: Sijo Poetry of Ancient Korea, adapted by Virginia Olsen Baron.
Copyright 1974 by Virginia Olsen Baron. Reprinted by permission of Henry Holt and Company.

Thanks to Ernestine Shargool for her translation of "Cincirinella."

Thanks to The Rockingham Press for "Morning Song," first published in MODERN PERSIAN POETRY,
edited and translated by Mahmud Kianush (1996).

Illustrations copyright © 2009 by Kay Chorao

Library of Congress Cataloging-in-Publication Data

Rhymes round the world / [compiled by] Kay Chorao.
p. cm.
ISBN 978-0-525-47875-1
Special Markets ISBN 978-0-525-42361-4 Not for resale
1. Children's poetry—Translations into English. 2. Children's
poetry, English. I. Chorao, Kay.
PN6109.97.R49 2009
821—dc22   2008013887

Published in the United States by Dutton Children's Books,
a division of Penguin Young Readers Group, 345 Hudson Street, New York, New York 10014
www.penguin.com/youngreaders

Designed by Irene Vandervoort

Manufactured in China
5 7 9 10 8 6 4

CONTENTS

I Am Like a Bear

I am like a bear,
I hold up my hands,
waiting for the sun to rise.

∽ Sung by Dog Chief
PAWNEE, NATIVE AMERICAN

CLOUDS IN THE SKY

The clouds in the sky
Have the funniest shapes
  Of lions
  And tigers
  And panthers
  And apes.
They twist and they turn,
And they split into two.
I'm sure that in heaven
There must be a Zoo.

              Old Jingle

Are You Sleeping?

Are you sleeping, are you sleeping?
Brother John, Brother John?
Morning bells are ringing,
    morning bells are ringing,
Ding dong ding,
    Ding dong ding.

Traditional Nursery Rhyme
FRANCE

Morning Song

In the shy blue sky
A bird cried:
"Where is it, then?
Where is the Morning?"

"It is on your wings,"
I said in reply.
And the bird flew away;
and the Morning bloomed
in my eyes.

Nader Naderpour
IRAN

Merrily, Merrily

Merrily, merrily
Shall I live now
Under the blossom that
Hangs on the bough.

⁓ William Shakespeare, The Tempest
ENGLAND

Wind Last Night

Wind last night blew down
A gardenful of peach blossoms.
A boy with a broom
Is starting to sweep them up.

Fallen flowers are flowers still;
Don't brush them away.

— *Anonymous*
KOREA

Give Me the Sky

Give me the sky
    For a playground.

Give me the sun
    For a ball.

Give me the rainbow
    To skip with,

And I'll never be naughty
    At all!

~ Anonymous

Lizzie

Lizzie Lizzie, spinning top,
Ever dancing, never stop.
Dancing in the morning dew,
Barefoot tap, one two, one two.

Lizzie, Lizzie, spinning top,
Ever dancing, never stop.
Dancing in the sun's warm rays,
Shining brightly at midday.

Traditional
POLAND

Pitter-patter

Pitter-patter, raindrops
　Falling from the sky;
Here is my umbrella
　To keep me safe and dry!

～ *Anonymous*

Slip on Your Raincoat

Slip on your raincoat,
Pull on your galoshes;
Wading in puddles
Makes splishes and sploshes.

～ *Anonymous*

Motherless Sparrow

Come here to me
and let's play together,
little motherless sparrow.

~ *Issa*
JAPAN

A Little Talk

The big brown hen and Mrs. Duck
Went walking out together;
They talked about all sorts of things—
The farmyard and the weather.
But all I heard was:
"Cluck! Cluck! Cluck!"
And *"Quack! Quack! Quack!"*
from Mrs. Duck.

~ *Mother Goose*

CINCIRENELLA

Cincirenella, his mule he would hire,
Hitched to his wagon she never would tire;
When she was harnessed with saddle and bridle,
Trit-trot, trit-trot, they never went idle.

So Cincirenella went speeding away,
Hundreds of miles he would ride every day;
When the night fell he would follow his star,
Trit-trot, trit-trot, he traveled afar.

Traditional
ITALY

ON THE STOOP

Sitting on the summer stoop,
Ice bars melting into soup.
Dripping, dropping,
Sticky, plopping,
Puddles almost never stay—
Kitty licks them all away.

K. Chorao
U.S.A.

Tickle Tickle

Me papa tickle me feet
he call it "finger treat"
me scream and run each time he come
me papa tickle me feet

he tickle me tummy, me chest, me arm
his fingers fly so wild
he say, "Come here, little man.
You my ticklin' chile."

he throw me high up in the air
and catch me from behind
me say, "Go higher!" and he say,
"Don't you know you're mine?"

me papa tickle me feet
he call it "finger treat"
me scream and run
(but OH, WHAT FUN!)
when papa tickle me feet.

Dakari Hru
AFRICA

Now Is the Month of Maying

Now is the month of Maying
When merry lads are playing,
    Fa la.
Each with his bonny lass
Upon the greeny grass.
    Fa la.
The Spring clad all in gladness,
Doth laugh at Winter's sadness.
    Fa la.

Thomas Morely
ENGLAND

Ring Around the Rosy

Ring around the rosy
A pocketful of posies
Ashes, ashes
We all fall down.

Nursery Rhyme
ENGLAND

Little Pine

My little pine tree is just a few feet tall.
It doesn't even have a trunk yet.
I keep measuring myself against it
But the more I watch it, the slower it grows.

Wang Jian
CHINA

NINETY-NINE

Ninety-nine years old!
How many candles does that make
On a birthday cake?
And when I went to school
My head would reach up to the ceiling;
A funny feeling.
Why am I only four?
All children want to be ninety-nine
    or more.

~ *Carolyn Hancock*
U.S.A.

Lower the Pinata

Lower the piñata,
Lower it a bit
So that they can give it
Another little hit!

Traditional
MEXICO

Hot Chocolate

One . . . two . . . three . . . hot!
One . . . two . . . three . . . chocolate!
One . . . two . . . three . . . hot!
One . . . two . . . three . . . chocolate!
Whip it up, hot chocolate!

Traditional
SPAIN AND MEXICO

Ten Fingers

I have ten little fingers
And they all belong to me.
I can make them do things.
Would you like to see?
I can shut them up tight
Or open them wide.
I can put them together
Or make them all hide.
I can make them jump high,
I can make them jump low,
I can fold them quietly
And hold them just so.

∽ *Anonymous*

The Shadow Rabbit

*T*he mother calls her child to see
    A shadow on the wall.
What is it? Why, a rabbit, dear—
    Mouth, ears and feet, and all!

    ~ Friedrich Froebel
    GERMANY

The Wheel
Around the World

If all the world's children
wanted to play holding hands,
they could happily make
a wheel around the sea.

If all the world's children
wanted to play holding hands,
they could be sailors
and build a bridge across the seas.

What a beautiful chorus we would make
singing around the earth,
if all the earth's children
would dance holding hands!

Traditional
MOZAMBIQUE

The Girl Wants to Dance

The girl wants to dance
    But she wears no shoes.
    I would give her mine,
    But they are old, and do not shine.

So I will take her to the cobbler's store
    Then she can dance, then she can soar
    Then she can stand, and she can sing
    A song with the sweetest happy ring.

~ *Traditional*
GREECE

Kookaburra

Kookaburra sits in the old gum tree,
Merry, merry king of the bush is he.
Laugh, Kookaburra! Laugh, Kookaburra!
Gay your life must be.

Kookaburra sits in the old gum tree,
Eating all the gum drops he can see.
Stop, Kookaburra! Stop, Kookaburra!
Leave some there for me!

Traditional
AUSTRALIA

The Indian Elephant

An Indian Elephant used for work
From honest toil he does not shirk.
All day long he'll push and shove,
While his owner guides him from above!
And when the hard day's work is done,
And downward goes the setting sun,
To the water they make their way,
To wash the mud off in the spray.

~ INDIA

Brown Owls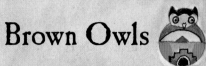

Brown owls come here in the blue evening,
They are hooting about,
They are shaking their wings and hooting.

ᔈ *Owl Woman, known as Juana Maxwell*
NATIVE AMERICAN

Day's End

*N*ight is come,
   Owls are out;
Beetles hum
   Round about.

Children snore
   Safe in bed;
Nothing more
   Need be said.

ᔈ *Henry Newbolt*
ENGLAND

Good night
ENGLISH

Goede nacht
DUTCH

Bonne nuit
FRENCH

Kalinishta
GREEK

Gute Nacht
GERMAN

Laila tov
HEBREW

Buona notte
ITALIAN

Jo tau
CANTONESE

Boas noites
GALICIAN

Oyasumi
JAPANESE

Anyong-hi jumuseyo
KOREAN

Shubha raatri
HINDI

Hanhepi waste
LAKOTA

God natt
NORWEGIAN

Dobroi nochi
RUSSIAN

Dobranoc
POLISH

Boa noite
PORTUGUESE

Buenas noches
SPANISH

This Little Light of Mine

This little light of mine
I'm going to let it shine
Let it shine, let it shine
LET IT SHINE

Traditional Spiritual
U.S.A.